Licensed exclusively to Top That Publishing Ltd
Tide Mill Way, Woodbridge, Suffolk, IP12 1AP, UK
www.topthatpublishing.com
Copyright © 2018 Tide Mill Media
All rights reserved
0 2 4 6 8 9 7 5 3 1
Manufactured in Zhejiang, China

Written by Carrie Hennon
Illustrated by Gareth Llewhellin

ISBN 978-1-78700-561-7

For the cutest buttons I know – Joshua and Phoebe.
With love from Aunt Carrie. x

Cute
as a
button

by Carrie Hennon

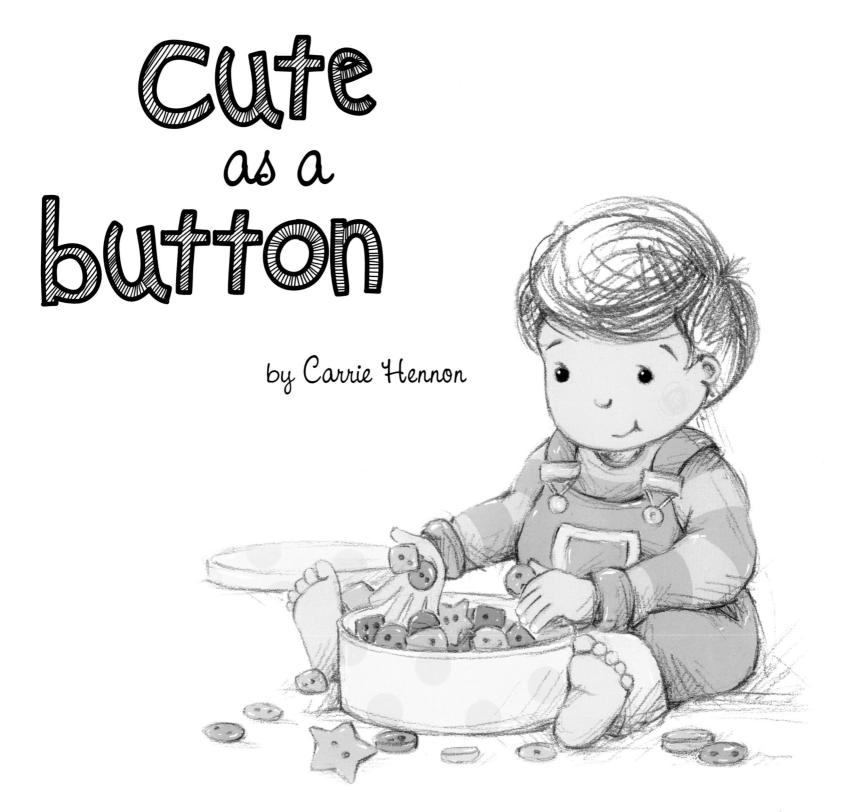

My Mommy had a big, round tummy.

It got bigger every day.

Mommy told me my little brother or sister was inside.

Daddy said Mommy was keeping baby safe and warm.

One morning,
when I woke up,
Grandma and Grandpa
were waiting downstairs.
Mommy and Daddy had gone
to the hospital in the night.

"Baby is on the way," said Grandpa.

I waited and waited for baby...
but babies take a long time!
I played with my toys but
they were no fun.

Then Daddy rushed in
with a big smile on his face.
"You have a baby sister," he said,
"and she's as cute as a button!"

"Cute as a button?" I thought.

"What does Daddy mean?"

Later, at bathtime,
Daddy played boats with me.

He washed me with a sponge
and lots of bubbles.
I looked down at my belly button...

"Cute as a button?" I thought.

"What does Daddy mean?"

The next morning at breakfast time, Daddy was talking on the telephone.

He was smiling and laughing.
"She's as cute as a button!"
he said.

"Cute as a button?"
I thought.

"What does Daddy mean?"

"What's cute about buttons?" I wondered.

I looked at the buttons on the clothes in the laundry basket. They didn't look cute.

I looked at the buttons on the washing machine. They had flashing lights—but they didn't look cute.

I looked at the television buttons.
I pressed them all at once,
and there was a funny noise...
but they didn't look cute.

Then I looked in Mommy's tin of buttons. There were lots and lots of buttons, all the colors of a rainbow. Maybe one of these buttons was cute.

But none of them looked cute to me.

Grandma and Grandpa came to visit again.
"We've been to see Mommy," Grandpa said,
"and we've met your sister."
"She's as cute as a button!" Grandma said.

"Cute as a button?" I thought.

"What does
Grandma mean?"

I didn't understand...
How could my baby sister be as cute as a button?
I couldn't find anything cute about buttons at all!

Then, **yippee!** Daddy brought Mommy home.

Mommy was carrying a bundle all wrapped in a blanket.

She bent down to show me what was inside.

I stretched up on tiptoe to see...

a tiny round face...

big shiny eyes...

soft dimpled cheeks...

I smiled at my baby sister
and said...